D1268877

IVAN AND THE INFORMER

IVAN AND THE INFORMER

By

MYRNA GRANT

MOODY PRESS

CHICAGO

ISBN: 0-8024-4189-0

Printed in the United States of America

For
Chris, Sue, Drew, and Jenni
with love and appreciation

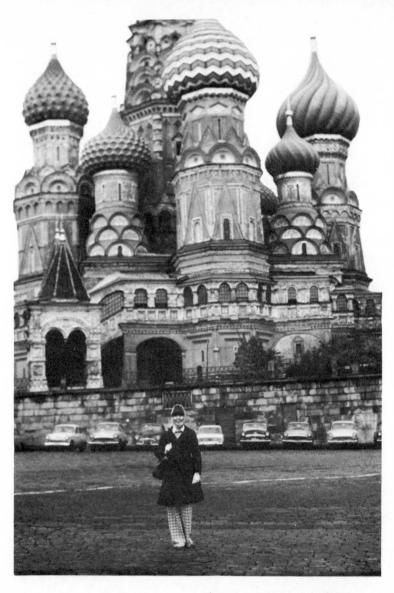

The author, Myrna Grant, during a recent visit to Russia, where this story takes place, poses in front of St. Basil's Cathedral in the Kremlin, Moscow.

Contents

Foreword

Ivan and the Informer is an accurate, moving story of the lives of two Russian children written by a perceptive author well informed on Christianity in Russia.

Problems of Christian young people in the Soviet Union are feelingly portrayed in the plot. As depicted in the story, Russia's atheistic government does not permit Sunday Schools or Christian youth gatherings. Training in communism and atheism, however, are mandatory for every Russian young person.

Ivan and the Informer will help boys and girls in the West understand the problems of Christian children behind the Iron Curtain. After reading this book, young people and adults will be prepared to pray more intelligently for their brothers and sisters in the Soviet Union.

PETER DEYNEKA, JR.

1

Trouble at School

IVAN NAZEROFF strode along the snow-filled Moscow street, trying hard to pretend that nothing had happened. Behind him, he could hear the running footsteps of his sister, Katya. Her heavy boots were thudding through snow that had been falling all day and was swirling like clouds of smoke around the hunched and hurrying people.

"Ivan! Wait for me!"

Ivan wondered how many times he had heard that call. Sometimes it was tiresome to be always waiting for a ten-year-old sister, two whole years younger than he. Today it was worse than tiresome. He wanted to think.

Katya's face was bright with cold as she laid a thickly-gloved hand on Ivan's coat sleeve to steady herself and catch her breath. "The bus was so crowded, I almost missed getting off," she gasped. "Didn't you wonder where I was?"

Ivan strode ahead, hoping his sister would not notice that he was upset. "Certainly not. You're much too old to have a brother leading you around. Besides, I saw you shoving your way off the bus."

11

Katya glanced quickly at her brother's stern face. "Why was Nickolai Fyodorovitch waiting for you after school today?" She asked the question with a stab of fear. She knew Nickolai had just had his fifteenth birthday and was a new member of the Komsomol, the Communist youth organization.

A gust of wind flung itself at the children, making them stagger against its force. Ivan fought ahead, pushing out his anger at Nickolai. He was grateful that the wind made it impossible to answer Katya.

But the turning of a corner gave them relief from the wind; and Katya, with her usual persistence, repeated the question.

"Same as always," Ivan finally answered. "He knows I am a Christian. He likes to make fun of me."

"But it wasn't the same," Katya retorted, her eyebrows tense with concern. "I saw him pushing you. He's a bully."

Ivan sighed. Katya had a way of persisting in her questions until she finally got the whole story, no matter what. "He said that as a Komsomol member he has a responsibility to make me see how stupid Christianity is. I told him I didn't have to listen to him, but he thinks he can make me."

"How will he make you?" The wind almost carried off Katya's words. "He can't *make* you listen!"

Ivan was trying not to think about it, let alone talk about it. But Katya's glance was insistent. "He's on the hockey team. The others know I am a Christian and say nothing. The coach knows, but he is interested in a good team and I am a good player. But if Nickolai protests my being on the team, the coach will have to remove me. After all, the team is for the Young Pioneers, and Christians don't belong to that!"

"But you have worked so hard! And it is such an honor to be chosen for the team. He's horrid!" Katya flung the words out with such indignation that an old woman, bent double as she slowly shoveled snow, stiffly raised her head and glanced briefly at Katya.

"We had an argument. I walked away. He would have come after me, but his bus was coming. He said he would be waiting for me after school tomorrow. He means to fight me."

Ivan pulled open the heavy door of the apartment building for his sister. It was a great relief to be in the long hallway and out of the wind and snow. He spoke quietly. "Say nothing of this to Momma, Katya. We don't want to worry her."

The wonderful smell of borscht greeted them as they entered their apartment.

"Momma, we're home!" Katya called, pulling off her boots with stiff fingers. Ivan sat down at the large table in the center of the living room, smiling as his mother bent to kiss him.

"What a cold day, children!" she exclaimed. "I have some hot tea ready for you. Katya, get the pot from the kitchen, please, and I'll bring out the glasses."

Ivan was glad this was a day his mother was home early from her job at the factory. He liked to smell the thick borscht soup already hot and to watch her steady hands laying out glasses and spoons and pouring the tea.

The children sat quietly, breathing the steam from the hot tea and feeling it warm their icy faces. Mother sat at the table with them, mending silently and smiling when she glanced at the two children. Katya sipped her tea slowly. She wanted to make it last, but Ivan was already beginning his homework, his glass set carefully beside his book.

It would be at least an hour, Ivan knew, before Father returned from his factory job, and in that hour Ivan could get a good start on what he had to complete for school tomorrow.

A good feeling settled upon Ivan. The threats of Nickolai seemed far away. The tension of being the only Christian in his classroom, the only one not to wear proudly the red neck scarf of the communist Young Pioneers, seemed less difficult. What if the others made fun of him? Here in this room, with the tea still warming him and the quiet face of his mother bending over her sewing, the tempests of life at school subsided. Ivan raised his head from his book to smile at Katya. He was sorry he had been so irritated with her after school. But as he glanced up, the soft lace curtains at the window across the room suddenly lifted as a blast of cold air swept in from the open front door. He turned in his chair with astonishment.

2

Poppa Loses His Job

"POPPA! What are you doing home so early from your job?" Ivan jumped to his feet and anxiously hung his father's heavy coat on the hook by the door.

Katya, with a tense face, sat still in her chair. Her eyes were on her mother. Katya had seen the look of fear that sprang to her mother's eyes as the door opened. But Momma was smiling at Poppa now. *Because Ivan and I are watching,* Katya thought.

"Poppa, are you sick?" Ivan persisted. His father, with a faint smile, sank wearily into his chair.

"Oh no, son! I am not sick." He sighed, looking at the concern on Momma's face. "It's nothing so bad. I was asked to leave my job at the factory. I am to report to the supervisor in the morning."

Momma sat opposite him and leaned toward him. Her voice was insistent. "But why?"

Poppa shrugged. "I don't know. Last week, one of the men beside me on the assembly line was asking me about Christianity."

17

"But Ivan, you were told so many times that you must not speak about religion at the factory."

Poppa shrugged. "I was answering his questions. That is permitted."

Katya burst out indignantly, "It is *supposed* to be permitted."

"He was my friend."

Mother went to the window and stared out. The room was quiet. "Christians have no 'friends' in Russia. You know that." The children could hear a tinge of weariness in her voice.

The face of Nickolai Fyodorovitch suddenly appeared in Ivan's mind. A tight feeling of fear returned to his chest, and he looked down at his school book still open on the table.

"We have other Christians for friends, Momma," Katya reminded her.

"Unless they are informers!" Ivan kept his eyes on his book as he answered Katya. He was immediately sorry he had spoken. It was unfair to mention informers when the family was already worried about Poppa's job. Informers were a hated part of Russian life. Found in every station of life, they bought the favor of the police by reporting on their fellow-workers, friends, and even their family members. An impulsive criticism of the government, the reading of a disapproved book, a fondness for foreign radio broadcasts— nothing was too small for an informer to use against others. Even in Christian groups there were informers, posing as believers and watching and listening for the chance to cause trouble. Ivan shuddered.

Momma broke the spell of sadness that was falling on the family. She turned from the window with a smile.

"Now, now, now. This is not so bad. Your father will

have an opportunity in the morning to explain to the supervisor that he was only answering his comrade's questions. I think we must pray."

Poppa gave Momma an appreciative smile as they clustered together for prayer. Poppa's voice rose and fell like a song. "Thanksgiving and praise to Almighty God," he was saying, "that I am counted worthy to bear this small concern for the sake of Jesus. Praise for the love of God, that could reach even to the supervisor. Praise for the forgiveness of God, that could give new life to the worker who reported me."

A feeling of sweetness touched Ivan, as it had many times before in prayer.

"Bring glory to the name of Jesus," Momma prayed.

Ivan silently agreed, and within himself added, *Even through me, Lord, if You want. Even through me.*

Momma gave Katya a playful spank. "Come! Let us set the table for supper!"

"Yes! Borscht!" Ivan declared enthusiastically. "It smells good, Momma."

Poppa inhaled the good borscht smell. "Of course it's good, Ivan. Your momma made it."

"I peeled the beets!" Katya declared, shaking out the tablecloth. "And I went to the shop especially for the sour cream. You should have seen all the lines today. It was no fun, I tell you! Waiting all that time just for sour cream!"

"Very good, Katychka!" Poppa tugged teasingly at the bow that caught Katya's two brown braids in a pretty loop at the back of her head. "Someday you will be as good a cook as your momma. Keep peeling the beets!"

They all laughed, Ivan louder than the rest.

19

It had been cold all day in the classroom, and Ivan wrapped his sweater tightly around himself and folded his arms, hugging himself for warmth. Usually he loved history, but today it was hard to listen to his teacher, Sophia Kutskova. His mind was on his father's factory and what was happening at the meeting with the supervisor. Sophia Kutskova was talking about the examinations which she had just handed back.

"Our leader, Lenin, would have been proud of your work, students. You have mastered some rather lengthy sections of Soviet history, and I, too, am pleased. It is important that you be able to follow the developments of all that went into our glorious revolution, even though these things seem to have happened very long ago."

The clock on the wall reminded Ivan that in a few minutes, school would be over, and perhaps he would have to confront Nickolai. He tried harder to concentrate on what his teacher was saying.

"In a very few years, many of you students will be proud to be in the Komsomol." Sophia Kutskova's eyes rested for an instant on Ivan, then moved away. "You will be happy, then, to have studied so diligently. Your history will mean even more to you when you all take your places in the service of your country in the Young Communist League." She paused before saying, "Now, you are dismissed."

Ivan gathered his books up quickly. *If only Katya is ready, perhaps we can hurry and avoid Nickolai,* he thought. He was startled to hear his teacher calling his name.

"Ivan Nazeroff, stay back. I wish to speak to you."

Ivan hurried to the front of the room. "Sophia Kutskova, may I tell my sister to go ahead without me? I expect I'll miss my bus."

His teacher smiled as she beckoned him to sit down.

20

"Your sister, no doubt, is a resourceful girl. I am almost certain she will be able to get her bus without you." She glanced at the open grade book on her desk. "You did well on your history examination."

Nickolai will not wait for me! Ivan thought happily. He smiled back at his teacher. "Thank you, Sophia Kutskova. I like history very much."

"I confess, I do not understand your behavior." The teacher frowned as she shook her head.

Ivan suddenly felt a pang of guilt. He tried to think what he could have done.

"You excel in history," Sophia Kutskova continued. "I sense in you a stirring of all that is fine in love for Mother Russia. And yet you will not wear the red neck scarf that shows you to be a loyal communist Young Pioneer."

"I'm sorry, Sophia Kutskova."

"We have talked together many times. You understand so much, Ivan. It makes me sorry to see you so stubborn and so set against me."

Ivan flushed. A flutter of fear tightened his voice. "I am not against you, Sophia Kutskova."

"Your parents are lost in the past. If they could see, they would know how corrupt and imperialistic their religious ideas are. They are clinging ignorantly to ideas that were cleaned away with the czars. But you are young, Ivan, and have the possibility before you of a great education."

She looked at Ivan expectantly. When he did not reply, she continued on the lecture Ivan had heard many times before, from many teachers. He began thinking again about his father's morning meeting with his supervisor at the factory. What had happened? If Poppa were fired, perhaps he would not be able to apply for another job.

"Why can you not see that you are throwing away your future for nothing? In years to come, no university will admit you if you cling to these fanatical ideas. I implore you to think about your future." Once again his teacher paused.

This time Ivan knew he must answer. "I do think about it, Sophia Kutskova."

The teacher smiled warmly. "Good. Then you will see that these uncultured ideas, this unscientific religious nonsense, cannot be for a young and progressive Soviet youth like you. It is only stupidity, Ivan. There is nothing ahead for you but trouble and suffering if you cling to religion. And for no reason!"

She stood, still smiling. Ivan stood also, and picked up his books. "Thank you, Sophia Kutskova. I know you have my interests at heart."

The teacher laid a small hand on his shoulder. "Of course I do." She paused and looked warningly at him. "And do you think it is easy for me to have one student in my class, as late in the year as this, who still refuses to wear the red scarf?"

Ivan suddenly felt cold.

3

A New Job

IVAN WALKED SLOWLY, trying to make the short block between bus stop and home last as long as possible. Feelings of relief and dread were struggling in his mind.

He was relieved that so far fifteen-year-old Nickolai had not carried out his threat to beat him up after school. Even the hockey practice today had been uneventful, although since Nickolai was the oldest boy on the team, his friendship with the coach worried Ivan. And today Nickolai had seemed to make as much of that relationship as possible. Time and again he had skated up to the coach, resting his stiffly-gloved hand on the coach's shoulder, suggesting plays, making little jokes, or listening to some confidence of the coach and nodding his head in agreement. But at least nothing bad had happened.

All the same, Ivan's steps were slow with dread. Perhaps Nickolai and his threats were unimportant, but what had happened to his father today at the meeting with his supervisor was important.

He tried not to think about the Christian fathers he knew

or had heard about who suddenly lost their work permits or who were arrested and sentenced to prison. Sometimes there were beatings by the police. Sometimes children were taken away from parents who were said by the police to be destroying their children's minds with religious superstition.

Ivan knew these things were not common; but, when a Christian citizen was noticed by the police for any reason, trouble often came of it.

There was no good smell of borscht today as Ivan opened the door of the apartment. The tearful face of Katya gazed at him. Ivan's heart sank.

Her voice was thick from crying. "Ivan! Where have you been? Poppa has been at the police station all day. Momma went there when I got home from school, to see if she could find out anything." Katya looked miserable, hunched in the dim winter light. Her schoolbooks were unopened on the table across the room.

"Sophia Kutskova kept me after school." Ivan switched on the light and unwound his knitted scarf.

"What did she want? Was it about Poppa?"

It took only a few moments for Ivan to repeat Sophia Kutskova's conversation with him. She had said the same things many times before. As Ivan finished, Katya again began to cry. Ivan sat on the arm of her chair. He wished Momma were home to comfort her.

"Everything is wrong, Ivan. None of the boys and girls in my class will be friends with me. I am called Katya, the stupid, or Katya, the grandmother, or Katya, the virgin Mary. I want to have friends like everyone else."

Ivan awkwardly handed her his handkerchief. "You have Christian friends," he tried.

26

"If I don't mind hiding to see them!" Katya blew her nose noisily. "And how often can we meet, anyway? It has to be someone's wedding or birthday or funeral, because it is so difficult to get permission to meet in groups. I want to be with a lot of friends, all together, and without worrying about the police!" She blew her nose again and began to feel better.

Ivan was thinking that perhaps they ought to pray for Poppa; but, before he could suggest it, the door swiftly opened and their parents hurried into the room, cold from the walk from the police station.

It had not been a bad time, really, Poppa said. At first the police had put him through the usual questioning. "Where do the Christians meet? Do any children attend the religious meetings?" Soviet law states that a person has to be eighteen before church attendance is permitted, so Poppa had been careful to explain that in his church, no children attended. Why was he trying to influence fellow workers to become Christians? Poppa had explained carefully, again, that he had only been answering his fellow worker's questions, since this was allowed by law.

Momma blew into the hot glass of pale tea that Katya had brought her. "But this time it was not the same as always. They brought the superintendent from the factory, and he accused your father of laziness and stealing!"

Poppa continued unlacing his heavy work boots. "It's almost funny. So many of the men take small things from the factory—a small tool, or some wood. The superintendent himself has carried off enough supplies to begin a small shop of his own. And *he* tells the police that *I* have been stealing."

Momma's voice was unsteady. "And to think you have never stolen so much as a minute from the factory!"

27

"But what about your job, Poppa?" Ivan was impatient to get to the point.

"It is not so bad. Not nearly so bad as I had feared."

Ivan noticed that Poppa was avoiding Momma's eyes and smiling at the children. "A new job, but I'll be home every night. I have been assigned to the State Collective Farm Number 462, outside of Moscow."

Katya jumped up and stamped her foot. Her dark eyes were flashing. "A farm worker! Oh! To do nothing wrong! To be honest and good, and to be punished! How glorious is our Mother Russia!"

Mother pushed Katya firmly into her chair. "Katya! I have spoken to you before about this. You must guard your thoughts and your tongue. You know the danger in speaking this way."

But Katya was still angry. "Perhaps Ivan is an informer!" she retorted.

"It is the *habit* of thought and speech that I fear," Mother continued sternly. "You must learn to discipline your thoughts!" She stared at Katya as if she would say more and then sighed. "Now you children have homework to do, and I have supper to prepare. Let's talk no more about this."

Later that night, Ivan lay awake in bed. The moon shone through the lace curtains at the window. His parents had talked and prayed long into the night, and the drone of their voices had made him drowsy. But now they were silent, and Ivan propped himself up on his elbow in bed and looked at the drifting moon.

It was unjust that his father, a trained factory worker, was assigned to a farm. His father had only answered a fellow worker's questions about Christianity. But the supervisor disliked believers and had chosen to report Poppa, and the police

28

had chosen to pretend to believe the lie about Poppa's stealing. The police, the supervisor, and Poppa all knew that the real reason Poppa was being sent to the farm was to make life difficult for him because he was a Christian.

Sophia Kutskova's words rang in Ivan's mind. *There is nothing ahead for you but trouble and suffering, if you cling to religion. And for no reason!*

The moon slipped behind a dense cloud, plunging the room into darkness. A few faint stars, not visible before, came into view.

How strange to think that simply believing in God could cause such troubles. For as long as he could remember, Ivan had known God existed. He could not imagine "changing his mind" to say he believed that there was no God. A person had only to look at the sky to know the wonder of God's creation!

But commitment to Jesus had not come easily to Ivan. When he had become old enough to understand the cost of being a believer in Russia, he had been afraid. Life was too exciting, too full of possibilities, to choose an outsider's life that would close so many important doors. Ivan smiled at the emerging moon as he remembered his determination to resist the call of Jesus Christ. It seemed so long ago.

His conversion had been simple, really. Ivan remembered walking in the forest last spring, in a world of green light and damp freshness. When he had gone into the forest, he had not been a Christian. When he had come out, he was. He tried to bring back what had happened to him in that walk, but it was a blur. His mind had been pulling in all directions; he remembered that. Then there had been a long time spent sitting against a tree. There had been an inner listening to some Bible verses Momma had taught him:

29

Come unto Me, all who are weary and heavy-laden, and I will give you rest.

Take My yoke upon you, and learn from Me, for I am gentle and humble in heart; and you shall find rest for your souls.

*I am the way, and the truth, and the life; no one comes to the Father, but through Me.**

There had been an inner argument, too. Then a warm sense of a Presence had come over him, and a word, "Come!" echoed in his heart. He had walked out of the forest with Christ. That part he remembered. And how Poppa had cried for joy! Poppa!

Ivan was fully awake now! How could he have lain, half-dreaming, forgetful of what awaited his father in the morning? Was it not a disgrace that a skilled factory worker would dig and carry on a farm? Poppa would have to leave Moscow on the earliest possible train and return to the apartment late. Was it not unjust? Ivan lay back on his pillow, staring at the ceiling. Morning would be a long time in coming.

*Matthew 11:28-29, John 14:6, New American Standard Bible.

4

Birthday Party

THE ARGUMENT had started slowly. Ivan had not meant to quarrel with his father. In fact, he had wanted to help him in some way. Ivan could see how tired and discouraged he was feeling after his first long day at the collective farm.

"Never mind, Natasha," Poppa had said to Momma. "Was not our Lord falsely accused? It is an honor to suffer for His sake."

It was not the words that had made Ivan feel a surge of love for his father. It was the playful way Poppa had smiled, as if comparing himself to the Saviour were a gentle kind of joke.

Poppa had eaten his supper hungrily, but without talking. When it was over, he called Ivan away from the last pages of his homework, talking softly because Katya was already in bed.

"You were planning, son, on meeting some of the boys from church this Sunday?"

Ivan had answered happily. It was his friend Alexi's birthday, and a perfect time for a few Christian boys to gather in

33

a home and have a Bible study without raising suspicion. But Poppa had been hesitant.

"Perhaps it would be best, this time, not to go. My trouble with the police—"

Ivan could tell by Momma's face that she agreed. She was clearing away Poppa's dinner plate and paused to listen to the conversation.

"But Poppa! No! I promised I would go. It is the only chance we boys have to be together and talk freely as Christians. They will think I am afraid if I don't go. They'll know you have been sent to the collective farm."

Poppa explained that it was not quite as important what one's friends thought as what the police thought. He explained again how careful Christians had to be not to draw attention to themselves in any way. He reminded Ivan of the police questionings that had occurred in the past. Perhaps because Ivan was, indeed, afraid of the police, he argued all the harder to be allowed to go.

In the end, Poppa had given permission, just before they gathered around the living room table for evening prayers. Ivan noticed that Poppa prayed longer than usual that his family would be safe and protected, and that they all would remain faithful disciples of the Lord Jesus Christ.

"Come in, Ivan! You're covered with snow!" With the exuberance of a boy newly turned fourteen, Alexi flung open the door. His high cheekbones were flushed with color, and his fair hair had been carefully combed for the occasion.

"Happy birthday, Alexi!" Ivan embraced his friend warmly, in the Russian manner. "My mother sends these cookies."

"Thank you!" Alexi slammed the door hard, oblivious to

34

the amusement of the other guests. "Off with your coat and boots, Ivan. You look frozen."

The cookies he held aloft, bearing them to the table with a flourish. Two boys, both older than Ivan, sat watching Ivan's entrance with smiles of pleasure. At the same time they followed with keen interest, the path of the cookies through the air.

"These we shall have with tea," Alexi declared. "And the little cakes Mother made for us."

"A feast!" Pyotr Kachenko was tall for his age, and sturdy. "Good peasant stock" he said of himself with satisfaction, and whether it was his height or his peasant stock that provided him with an astonishing appetite, no one knew.

But Alexi whisked the cookies to a safe distance, placing them in front of Fyodor Sakovich. Fyodor was Pyotr's opposite. Small for fifteen, and slight of build, he was the pride of his family because of his athletic ability and excellent grades at school. That he was somewhat nervous, as well, accounted for his pushing the cookies even farther down the table from Pyotr's enthusiasm, meanwhile greeting Ivan with a wave of his free hand.

Alexi emerged from the kitchen, carrying a small tea tray with glasses clinking crazily against each other. On a side table in the room sat a brass samovar, the family's prized possession. Its surface was cloudy with steam from the scalding tea inside. With gusto, Alexi began pouring the tea and handing around the glasses.

"Looks more like a real birthday party this way! It's always best to be on the safe side, brothers!"

Ivan smiled at his friend. "It *is* a birthday party, Alexi. I do wish you many happy birthdays to come."

The other boys added their greetings until Alexi was beaming with embarrassed pleasure and passing the cakes and cookies insistently, even though he had secretly hoped to have some left over for bedtime.

Bible study posed a major problem for the boys, as it does in most small study groups in Russia. The Bible, for a brief time plentiful in Russia following World War II, had been a despised book for over twenty-five years. No Bibles were printed, none were sold in book shops or secondhand stores, and the few that existed were worn and treasured volumes, often used by a large group of believers or a whole church. None of the boys or their families had Bibles. Christian radio broadcasts in Russia, beamed from foreign countries, provided the Christians with some Scripture. What was heard on the radio or in church was carefully copied into notebooks and shared with friends. By this means, a quantity of Scripture could be accumulated, but it was woefully small.

Today, in preparation for the birthday, Alexi had obtained some Scripture from a recent radio broadcast. With a sense of achievement, he pulled a folded paper out of his pocket.

"This Scripture I have is from Jeremiah!" He opened the paper and set it carefully on the table in front of him. "Some of it in the middle I missed, because Masha fell out of bed and made a great racket, and I couldn't hear."

Pyotr banged the table uproariously. "Radios should come with ropes for tying up little sisters! In my case, chains for our Sonya." The exploits of Pyotr's tiny sister Sonya were notorious. "But never mind, let's get on with what you have."

Soon the boys were absorbed in the words of Alexi's paper. A discussion about what is left behind when one follows Christ ensued.

Pyotr's merry eyes became grave when he talked about his dream of continuing his piano lessons. "My teacher says I am good enough to play here in Moscow, someday, if I could keep on. But of course, I am not a member of the Komsomol, so advanced lessons are impossible."

"It is sports that I miss." Fyodor spoke in a low voice. The boys knew how much gymnastics meant to him.

But Fyodor brightened and smiled with a shrug. "Once when I was small, I was in a physical culture show at Dynamo Stadium. That is something to remember! There were hundreds of us on the field; and when we finished, a great curtain of water jets shot to the sky. It was wonderful! But of course, the Organization of Sports Societies does not permit entrance to anyone not in the Komsomol. Now that I am fifteen and should have joined, that is over for me."

"But the Lord will repay you, Fyodor," Alexi reminded him gently.

"No question of that. But it is hard."

As the youngest boy in the group, Ivan said little. It was enough to be with Christian friends, feeling the warmth of their mutual affection and concerns. The awkward, tight feeling that closed in on him at school, where he was thought peculiar, was completely gone. He loved to bend his head over the same paper that absorbed the other boys and join with them in prayer. Ivan wished the afternoon could go on forever.

It was Fyodor who had to leave first. They had finished their study and prayers, and were singing softly some of the church hymns their parents had taught them. Pyotr led enthusiastically. Ivan was smiling as he sang. He could not help it, and the smiles on the other boys seemed to reflect his own joy.

But Fyodor had to leave. There was a flurry. Somehow Alexi had lost his paper with the Scripture among the empty glasses and plates on the table, or among the coats piled on the chairs. Fyodor helped to look for it as long as he could, but finally, cramming his gloves into his pockets and leaving his coat unbuttoned in his haste, he left with hurried apologies and birthday wishes.

It was pleasant for the three remaining boys to sit together discussing school and their teachers and the hockey teams. Pyotr and Alexi thought Ivan should not worry about Nickolai and his threats. The coach had already shown that he wanted to overlook the fact that Ivan was not a member of the young communist group, Young Pioneers. That should reassure him. And besides, Ivan was a very good player! Pyotr rumpled Ivan's hair affectionately. And it should not be too hard to stay away from Nickolai after school. Fyodor was in his class at school and would try to detain him by chatting.

Painfully soon, the time came for Ivan to leave, if he were to hope to get home in time for supper. Pyotr had been invited to stay for supper with Alexi, and was already singing loudly as he began to help clear up the room before Alexi's parents returned. Ivan shrugged into his coat regretfully. It had been a wonderful afternoon. His heart sang with Pyotr's tune as he ran lightly down the apartment stairway to the front door.

If he had known what was waiting for him, he would not have been whistling as he opened the door and stepped out into the darkening street.

5

Police Questioning

IVAN WAS INTENT on peering down the road to see if a bus was coming through the foggy Moscow twilight. At first he did not see the two men moving out of a doorway toward him.

He began to run as the dim lights of the bus appeared, moving carefully through the cold mists.

"Ivan Nazeroff?" Ivan was startled as the two figures squarely blocked his way. In an instant he knew they were members of the secret police. His heart beat wildly.

"Yes?" How could they know his name?

"Where are you coming from?"

Ivan's tongue seemed frozen in his mouth. The bus lumbered slowly past him, its headlights catching the three figures by the edge of the street, then moving on.

The taller of the two men, a disciplined, soldierlike figure, took Ivan's arm. "You have some questions to answer, Ivan Nazeroff. We will go to the police station and see what we can straighten out."

Squeezed between the two officers in the small police car, Ivan stared at the seat in front of him. He did not dare turn

41

his head to look out of the wide windows. The tall policeman was sitting erect, glancing at his watch and out into the winter mist. The other officer had leaned his head against his window and appeared to be going to sleep.

Ivan clenched his hands together in his lap in an effort to gather strength for what lay ahead. If only Poppa were with him! He pictured the scene at home: Katya setting the table and Momma bringing in the plates of bread and soup, perhaps glancing out the window to see if he were coming.

With eyes open, Ivan began to pray. It was hard to concentrate in the lurching of the car, as it slowed for intersections and then sped up. Ivan was anxious not to appear to be praying. He tried to tighten the muscles in his face into a stern expression.

The car slid to a quiet stop. The tall officer, Grigory Yakov, sprang out, holding the door for Ivan. The three walked briskly through the iron entrance gates and into the bright light of the police station. They entered a small room where the men began removing their coats. Ivan took his coat off as he was directed, his heart pounding.

Comrade Yakov sat down behind a small desk, pen in hand.

"Comrade Ivan Nazeroff, where were you this afternoon" His voice was patient and not unfriendly.

"At a birthday party. At the home of Alexi Petrovitch. I've done nothing wrong."

The second officer lazily lit a cigarette and stood in front of Ivan. "Yes. You were at the home of Alexi Petrovitch. Perhaps it was his birthday. Perhaps it was something else, as well." He blew a puff of smoke toward the ceiling. "What did you do at the home of Alexi Petrovitch?"

"We had a birthday party. We had tea and cookies that

my mother sent, and cakes." Ivan's heart was beating more quietly now. It helped to be able to talk. *Saviour,* he was praying silently, *help me to know what to say.*

"And who else was at this home this afternoon?" The first officer raised his pen.

"It was a birthday party. Alexi Petrovitch, my friend, was fourteen."

"Who else was present?" Comrade Yakov frowned. He did not like to repeat himself.

Ivan sat staring at the pen in Comrade Yakov's hand. If it were only a birthday party, why would he not tell the names of those present? To refuse would be to admit that something illegal had taken place. In a low voice he gave the names of his friends, insisting, "It was a birthday party."

But the interrogation was just beginning. A long line of questioning followed, concerning his school, his father's job, his mother's job, the names of every friend he could remember, where his family had lived before coming to their present apartment, his teacher's name, his grades, his sister's grades, her friends. Ivan began to feel light-headed from the stuffy room and hunger. He had not eaten supper, even if the police had. Did Ivan have a Bible? Did he know what Jeremiah meant? Did he ever attend church?

It seemed that hours had passed, when the two men abruptly stood and left, locking the door of the small room behind them. They gave no explanation, and Ivan was afraid to ask what was to happen next. As the door quickly opened and closed for the men, Ivan's heart lurched as he thought he glimpsed a boy in the hall—perhaps two boys.

After a long interval, the officers returned. Ivan thought they appeared pleased; there was a lightness in their manner, although their faces remained professionally severe. More

43

questions followed, this time along a different and more alarming line.

Was it possible that his father was religious? What church did he attend? Was his mother a Christian believer? Was he? His sister? The answers burned in his throat and he could feel a trickle of perspiration lying above his lip and running down the sides of his face. Again the questions returned to the birthday party, and Ivan repeated the answers he had given earlier. There was a pause. Putting his hand inside his pocket, Comrade Yakov slowly pulled out the small piece of paper on which Alexi had written his verses from Jeremiah.

Ignoring the paper, and asking the question as if he did not know the answer, Comrade Yakov leaned toward Ivan. "At this 'birthday party,' a paper was passed around. What was on the paper?"

Ivan's eyes were hypnotized by the white paper in the officer's hand. Angrily, Comrade Yakov shouted the question. Ivan tried to steady his hands, which were shaking violently on his knee.

"Verses from Jeremiah." What would happen to him? He knew of older Christian boys who had been beaten by the police.

"What is that? Jeremiah?" The short officer was smoking again, and he spat out his words.

Suddenly Ivan could almost see his father as he was when he had come home from his interview at the police station only days earlier. As clearly as if his father were beside him speaking, Ivan heard the words, "It is an honor to suffer for His sake." Ivan took a steadying breath.

"It is a part of the Bible, comrade. It is a part of the Old Testament."

There was a long pause. Ivan felt a stillness in the room

that had not been there before. *Perhaps it is my own fears that are still,* he thought. It was true that he had stopped trembling, and he raised a hand to push his wet hair off his forehead.

"That is all for the present. You may go home now." Comrade Yakov's voice seeemed to boom out of a vacuum. Ivan could not believe what he was hearing. But the police left immediately, leaving the door open behind them as their footsteps rapidly faded.

As he stood, Ivan realized he was weak. A cold blast of air from the corridor made him begin to shake as he quickly pulled on his coat. The hall was dark and empty, and the desk in the front office of the station was also empty as he hurried past it and outside. From the appearance of the streets, Ivan knew it was late. With relief he saw that the police station was on a major subway route. Knees still shaking from his ordeal, he found his way to a subway station entrance, grateful that he still had his bus fare in his coat pocket. An old woman mopping the subway platform with a filthy mop glanced at him in surprise. Ivan was sure, then, that it was very late.

6

Accused

IT SEEMED STRANGE that life continued in the ordinary way the next day. The evening at the police station had been so extraordinary that somehow Ivan was surprised that the streets of Moscow were unchanged and that the hours at school passed as if nothing had happened to him at all.

Returning home so late the night before and seeing every window in his parent's apartment lit in the darkened building had given Ivan a peculiar sensation. Such a feeling of exhaustion had overcome him that it had been hard to force himself up the stairs, even though he was longing for food and bed and was eager to relieve his family's fears.

But today, in spite of an odd feeling of tiredness, all seemed as before.

Perhaps it was because Ivan was dozing over his homework after school that he was so startled by Poppa's unusually early arrival from work. Poppa seemed suddenly to be in the room, the door still open behind him. He laughed at their astonishment, swinging Katya in his arms and making her shriek like a baby. Momma stood watching smiling in won-

47

der. Bewildered, Ivan closed the door. His mind was hazy with sleep, but he knew it was much too soon for Poppa to be home from the collective farm.

Gathering the family to the table, Poppa collapsed breathlessly on a chair, his coat undone but still on. He laughed away their excited questions and began to speak. "This morning at the train station, as I was waiting to go to the farm with all the other workers, a police car pulled up and the comrade officer called me over."

Ivan saw his mother's folded hands tighten, but Poppa's face remained cheerful. Clearly, the story was a good one.

"I was told to get in to be driven to the subway, where I could get transportation to my factory! I was told to report to my old job at the factory, and that is where I have worked all day!"

Momma's eyes were wet. "Praise to our glorious God!"

"Yes!" At Poppa's leading, the small family stood in a circle, heads bowed, and praised God for His working to restore Poppa's job. So unusual was such a reversal of a police order, each knew that God had brought it to pass. Katya's voice was blurred with tears. She was asking for forgiveness for the bitterness she had held in her heart toward the injustice of the government. Ivan, too, felt regret for the fear that had gripped him last night in the police interview. Should he not have known that God would take care of him? But to do such a wonderful thing! To restore Poppa's job!

Smiles of joy remained on the family's faces throughout the evening. Katya finished her homework early enough to read. Apparently all was well with the world.

Ivan tried not to think about the questions that were nagging at his brain. *Why was Poppa given his job back?* There was something about it that did not seem to fit. He tried to

48

concentrate on his homework but his train of thought was constantly interrupted by a flood of questions. All day he had watched at school for Alexi or Pyotr or Fyodor. There was little comfort in the fact that because they were older, their classes were in another part of the building. Often they managed to pass him or wave to him across the courtyard. He was worried that he had not seen any one of them all day. Were they not at school? Were they being held by the police? And how had the police known about the meeting? How had they obtained the paper with the Bible verses? His head swam and buzzed over his books, and then everything was quiet. From a long distance away he could hear Momma's voice.

"Ivan. No more homework! You must go to bed. You had so little sleep last night!" He awoke with a feeling of great grogginess. Poppa's arms were helping him up from his chair and leading him to the bedroom. Almost in a dream, he undressed and fell into bed. The feeling that something was not right remained with him.

Snow fell all the next day. The students in Moscow School Number 17 were accustomed to seeing it pile up on the sills of the narrow windows until it almost blocked their view of the sky. Ivan's day was going well. Last night's sleep had greatly refreshed him, and the events of the Sunday night police questioning seemed far away now. Perhaps nothing more would come of it. Still, Ivan's eyes scanned the halls and courtyards for a glimpse of one of his Christian friends.

Sophia Kutskova praised Ivan as he gathered up his books and slipped them into his schoolbag.

"I am happy to see you working so hard, Ivan." She smiled, her eyes resting on the collar of his shirt. He knew she was

49

silently reminding him that he ought to be wearing the red neck scarf of the communist Young Pioneers.

"There is to be an all-Moscow intermediate history competition in the spring. Examinations will be given, and chosen students from all the schools will be asked to write a historical essay. You have the best grades in our classroom, Ivan. I would like to choose you to represent our class, and indeed, the intermediate school." She hesitated. "Of course, I can hardly choose a student of history who cannot proudly wear his own country's red scarf." She smiled again. There was a pleading in her eyes that made Ivan uncomfortable. "You could win for our school, Ivan. I know it. Over every other school in Moscow! Please think about what I am saying."

Ivan's boots were noisy as he hurried along the hall. In a group of students ahead, Katya could be seen with a classmate. Ivan knew she would be so happy to have a friend that she would not want to ride the bus with him. The two girls were bending over an open book as they walked. Ivan laughed to see them bumping into students as they went along.

Outside, the wind stung his face, and he licked his snowy lips with his tongue. Some boys were sliding on the ice in the schoolyard, while others were throwing fluffy snowballs and shouting with laughter as they exploded softly on the coats of their classmates. Ivan stopped abruptly as he heard his name called. It was Pyotr, pushing between students, his breath puffing in front of him as he ran, and his blond hair wet against his forehead.

A handful of snow Pyotr had scooped up as he ran hit Ivan softly on the chest, bursting in all directions in a spray of white.

"You want a snowball fight, do you, Pyotr Kachenko?"

50

Ivan called with joy. Pyotr was beside him now, catching his breath and frowning. His voice was guarded.

"Stay over here a bit, away from the other. Keep the snowballs coming. I want to talk to you."

It would be safer, of course, if they were not seen together for too long. Pretending to have a snowball fight was a good idea, but Pyotr looked very serious. Ivan began to feel fearful. He could see that Pyotr was upset.

It seemed that all the boys were taken that Sunday night to the police station. All had been questioned and finally released. Fines of fifty rubles each had been assigned to the parents of the boys, for permitting them to attend an illegal youth meeting, and their names had been placed on a police reactionary list.

Ivan wondered why his parents had not been fined. Fifty rubles! That was a lot of money!

Pyotr was wondering about the paper with the verses from Jeremiah. How had the police obtained this? Ivan agreed that it was incomprehensible. But Pyotr continued. With a bewildered feeling, Ivan realized that Pyotr was pointing the question at him.

In a flash, Ivan's head seemed to clear. He understood the uneasy questions that had been with him since Sunday. An informer! There would have to have been an informer in order for the police to have known about the Bible study at Alexi's house!

He could hardly bring himself to put the thought into words. Catching a gloveful of snow and tossing it, he stepped a little closer to Pyotr.

"Could there have been—an informer, Pyotr?"

Pyotr's expression did not change into the astonishment

51

Ivan had expected. He crossed his arms and thrust out his chin, observing Ivan coolly.

"I was going to ask you that question, Ivan Nazeroff."

Ivan stared in horror at the accusing face of his friend. He, the informer? Surely Pyotr could not even think that he would do such a thing! Suddenly he felt as if he were with a stranger. He stammered as he spoke.

"But Pyotr! How can you think—that? Why-why would I do such a thing?"

The older boy's face remained unchanged. "I wonder how many rubles *your* family had to pay, Ivan." Seeing Ivan's confused expression, he continued contemptuously, "You told us on Sunday that your father had lost his job at the factory and had to do unskilled labor at the state collective farm. Yet everyone knows that he has his old job back. Why would such a nice thing happen to your father, Ivan Nazeroff?" Pyotr spit out Ivan's two names in disgust.

Ivan could not face the indignant stare of the older boy. His eyes dropped to the snow at his feet as he answered, "I do not know, Pyotr Kachenko. But I promise you, it had nothing to do with me. You must not think I was the informer."

But the boots of Pyotr Kachenko were already marching swiftly away from Ivan. Pyotr had not waited for an answer.

7

A Proposition

IT WOULD HAVE BEEN easier if Ivan had told his parents. Poppa would have prayed for him, his heavy arm around Ivan as they knelt together. After a lifetime of injustices, he would know what to say to Ivan.

But the pain that Momma would carry in her eyes! He had seen it so many times. From as far back as he could remember, it had been there on Sunday mornings when she kissed the children before leaving for church. How she wanted them to be allowed to attend! But this was against the law, and Momma was careful not to deliberately break a law.

The pain was there when Katya was mocked at school for being a Christian. When she was very small, Katya had wept and insisted she was never going back. Katya had learned, for the most part, not to cry anymore. She, too, saw how her tears made Momma suffer.

Ivan remembered how Momma had paced the floor the night Poppa had lost his job at the factory. She had said little, but her quiet voice had been shaking as she prayed. Ivan had been shocked. But Momma had smiled at the chil-

55

dren after prayers, and had given them bread and butter at bedtime.

It would have been easier to tell, perhaps, but Ivan would not do it. His parents had enough worries of their own.

But it was lonely. Only for an hour or two every day did Ivan forget that his friends thought him to be an informer. Bent over his hockey stick, skimming the ice, slamming the puck to his teammates, Ivan thought of nothing except the game, the net and the score. It was thrilling to be chosen for the team, and a grateful glance from a teammate as he shot him the puck or a word of encouragement from the coach pushed him into playing as never before.

Nickolai Fyodorovitch was a brilliant goalie, moving constantly, crouching in the net, swaying from side to side, his eyes never leaving the puck. Soon the league games would begin. Nickolai was sure to be chosen. So far Nickolai had not made an issue of the fact that, as a Christian, Ivan belonged to no communist organization. But when the league games sponsored by the Komsomol began, would he then begin an outcry against Ivan?

In the locker room, Ivan watched him move from friend to friend, laughing, and making his way to the coach to tell some joke that brought an amused smile to the lips of the older man. Every other member of the school team was also a member of the Young Pioneers, or had just turned fifteen and joined the impressive Komsomol. They knew each other well from the club meetings, and Ivan envied the boys' easy friendliness with one another. He threw his skates in his locker and shyly made his way out of the locker room and into the biting Moscow cold.

It seemed a long time since he had seen Alexi or Pyotr or Fyodor. He did not blame them for avoiding him, since they thought he was an informer. They had to be cautious. Their families had already been heavily fined. Why would they continue to be friends with a person whom they thought had informed?

The wind wailed between the buildings. Ivan felt miserably alone. He had to tell someone!

Katya was curled up in Poppa's chair and reading her geography notes. She was trying to memorize the major towns east of the Ural mountains, and she barely looked up as Ivan flung himself into the apartment.

"Katya!"

She lowered her book, surprised by the urgent note in Ivan's voice.

"I've got to talk to you! I'm in trouble."

Katya's half smile faded into concern. She uncurled her legs and sat on the edge of Poppa's chair as Ivan drew up a wooden chair from the big table beside her.

"What trouble?" Katya's mind was racing.

"I can't tell Poppa and Momma. They have enough troubles of their own. But it doesn't make sense."

Katya strained to follow the conversation.

"Poppa is fired from his job at the factory and told he must work as a farmer in the collective outside of Moscow." His voice was thoughtful. "That Sunday I participate in a Christian meeting with my friends. Someone reports all of us. The next day, Poppa has his job back at the factory, and we are not even fined, although the other boys' families are. I just don't understand."

Katya shook her head in impatience. "*I* don't understand what *trouble* you're in. Do you mean that questioning by the police?"

57

"Of course not. I've been questioned before."

"Then what?"

Ivan still talked slowly, his eyes searching Katya's face for reactions.

"Someone informed. Right, Katya?"

"Yes!" her voice was impatient.

"The boys think it was me." His words came in a rush. "So that Poppa could get his job back at the factory. They think I went to the police and confessed and offered their names because of Poppa."

Katya's expression froze.

"Your friends told you they think *you* are an *informer?*" Her shock melted into anger. "It is a shame that they could think such a thing!"

Ivan smiled at her loyalty. "No. It is logical. There was no other way for the police to know, except through an informer." What he was saying suddenly chilled him to the bone. "Katya! *I* am not the informer! But one of the other boys *is!*"

The children sat in silence for a moment. The enormity of the idea overwhelmed them.

"It couldn't have been anyone else," Ivan repeated in wonder. "The police had been given the piece of paper with Scripture on it that we used at the meeting. It had to be someone who had been there. Katya, I've been so upset about being accused of informing, I never till this moment realized that the real informer would have to be Pyotr, Fyodor, or Alexi."

"Well, you'll never find out who did it, so what's the use of worrying?" Katya looked bleak. There were so many disappointments in life.

Ivan paced the floor impatiently. "Don't you see? Everyone thinks I am the informer, so they will be careful about me. But the real informer will move about freely, picking up all the information he wants and passing it along to the police."

"Oh Ivan! Tell Poppa! I'm scared."

Ivan paced restlessly to the window and back, unable to keep his body still while his mind was so active. In less than an hour, Momma would be home. Ivan was thankful that there was that much time before she was to arrive. He glanced out at the street as if to assure himself that she was not coming. What he saw drained the color out of his face.

"Katya!" His heart was pounding. "Sit down and pretend to do your homework."

She obeyed instantly.

"The police who questioned me last Sunday are turning into our building."

Katya began to cry in fear.

"They may not be coming here. Katya, you must not look afraid."

There was efficient pounding on the door.

The two officers looked exactly as they had before. Their eyes swept the small apartment as they entered. No, it did not matter that the parents were not yet home from work. It was Ivan they wished to speak to. It would be convenient, perhaps, for little sister to wait in another room? This did not concern her.

Ivan admired Katya's dignity as she picked up her book and went into the bedroom, closing the door behind her with a respectful smile at the police. He could imagine how she would be sitting, trembling on the bed. He knew she was praying.

Ivan was astonished that the two police knew he was suspected of being an informer. And they had been at his school checking his grades. How Sophia Kutskova would have assured them she was doing everything she could to draw Ivan away from the superstition of his parents. But what was this about Lenin?

Comrade Lutsgov's voice remained friendly.

"I see from your school records you are following our great leader Lenin's advice when he said, 'Study, study and study!' "

"Yes, comrade." Ivan felt uncomfortable. Things were going to be serious if they were bringing Lenin into it.

"You do follow the teachings of Lenin, then?"

"Some of them. You know I am a Christian." It was Lenin who had said, "Religion is the opiate of the people."

The short officer sighed impatiently. "We do not think this childish Christian play will last long. We have already written down your name in a file with those of the other fanatics in Soviet society. You are just a boy, and yet your name is with those who resist the glorious new world our leader Lenin called us to."

Comrade Yakov put an arm around Ivan's shoulders. Ivan tried not to stiffen. "It is not too late for you, Ivan Nazeroff. We need intelligent boys like you to serve Mother Russia. We can see to it, Ivan, that you can play hockey on any teams you're good enough for." Ivan's heart lurched. "But I think it is history, also, that you love. We can give you entrance to whatever university you qualify for, in years to come, if you will put aside this foolish Christian fairy tale and help us. You could become a great historian someday."

Ivan was torn between wishing his mother would come home and fearing that the door would open and she would be there.

"Don't you want to continue your education?"

60

Ivan swallowed. "Yes, comrade. With all my heart."

"But you know very well it will be almost impossible for you to go to the university if you are not a member of the Young Communist League."

"But I cannot." Ivan hoped he sounded respectful.

"Of course you can." The officer drew him to the sofa, and together they sat down. The short officer stood smoking by the window.

"That is why we are here. You can stay within your group of believers. Go to little meetings like last Sunday's, as before. From time to time, answer some questions for us about the other Christians. You will not have to join the Communist party openly. You will nobly serve our glorious motherland. Ivan, already your 'Christian' friends have turned against you."

The second officer suddenly smiled. "We can see to it that they no longer will believe that you are the informer. It would be necessary to remove that impression!"

"How could you do that?"

"How?" the officer choked on his smoke, coughing good naturedly and stubbing out the cigarette. "By letting it leak out who the real informer is. These things are easily arranged."

It would be a truly wonderful thing, Ivan thought, no longer to be suspected. And for the real informer to be found out! The whole church would be safer then.

Comrade Yakov sighed. "If we were not concerned for you, Ivan Nazeroff, if we did not care about your future, why would we come here? You are our young comrade. A great future can be yours. We are extending to you the hand of brotherhood. Join us!"

8

A Bad Day

THEY HAD GIVEN him a week to decide. Ivan tossed on his bed night after night, his mind a storm of thoughts. Perhaps he could pretend to cooperate with the police. Then the real informer would be exposed as they promised. It might be that he could give worthless information to the police. But could he? They would find out. What would happen to him then?

Walking to school, Ivan imagined his coming meeting with the police. If he refused, they would no longer have reason to be patient with him. Would he be beaten? A cold fear swept over him. It had happened that in some cases, Christian children were removed from their parents for "reeducation." What if he were sent away to a state home for the children of reactionaries?

And how would he ever become free from the label of *informer?* One of the other boys was guilty, perhaps every day giving information to the police without any fear of suspicion. Ivan pictured him listening to conversations of

Christians and taking down names of new believers or the travels of some of the preachers. He shuddered in disgust.

He had told Katya only that the police has questioned him again. He was glad for the thick door between the living room and bedroom. If she had heard the police asking him to inform, she would have immediately told their parents when they returned from work. As it was, he had enough trouble persuading her that nothing would be gained by worrying them about a second questioning.

It was the Christian radio broadcasts from overseas that night that gave Ivan a measure of peace. For as long as he could remember, the family had gathered in the evening before the shortwave radio set, which was standard equipment in Russian homes.

"Come Katya. Come Ivan, come!" His mother would call them, flapping her apron in their direction as if she were shooing chickens into a barn. Poppa had the chair beside the radio. Ivan sat on the arm of it and Katya at Poppa's feet. Momma was by her basket of mending on the table, her fingers sometimes becoming still as she listened to the message.

Momma never needed to hurry them to the radio. Like most Christian children in Russia, overseas Christian broadcasts were the only religious education they ever had, other than the teachings of their parents. And their parents did not have the reverenced book called the Bible from which to teach them. The radio voice had a Bible.

The radio preacher was talking about a man, Daniel, who was sentenced to death in a den of many hungry lions. Daniel had refused to obey the wrong laws of his government. Katya nodded knowingly when the radio preacher talked about the government. Katya never missed an opportunity to point out, even in a gesture, the unfairness of the Soviet government. Momma tipped her head disapprovingly at Katya.

But God had not let Daniel be harmed. By a miracle, he had closed the jaws of the lions, and Daniel had not been eaten. Ivan listened closely.

"I am innocent before God," Daniel had declared to his king. That was why he had been safe from the lions. God had protected him.

Would God protect me from the anger of the police if I refused to inform? Ivan wondered to himself. The radio pastor continued with his sermon, but Ivan was left behind in his thoughts. Quietly a *yes* seemed to grow within him. God *would* protect him! His spirit lifted in a freedom he had not felt for a long time. He smiled as he caught his father's eye.

But God had not spoken to him about Sophia Kutskova, Ivan thought grimly, as he recopied a history chart for his teacher. Nothing he could do these days seemed to satisfy her. She had not mentioned to him that the police had asked her questions about Ivan. But her impatience with him seemed to grow day by day. She had begun to make teasing remarks to the class about Ivan's Christianity. She had never done this before.

Today she was angry. Why could Ivan not understand the most simple directions? Perhaps all the religion he had collected into his head was festering there and making ordinary thought impossible. A ripple of laughter passed over the class. Ivan stared at his desk, his face red from embarrassment and anger.

Later she stood next to his desk, speaking to the class in a grieved tone. "Ivan does not wish to represent our school in the all-Moscow history contest." Helplessly Ivan sat with his head lowered, desperately fighting back tears of disappointment and frustration at the news. "Perhaps, if he wanted, he could win for us. But such things do not interest him, I am afraid. It may be that he is too busy praying to God to work on such an earthly thing as a history essay for the honor of his school." Ivan could feel the baleful glances of his classmates.

It was hard to have his hopes dashed so suddenly. He had been secretly dreaming that perhaps Sophia Kutskova would permit him to enter an essay in the contest, even if he was not a member of the Young Pioneers. There were no official rules against it. Of course, if he should win, his victory would be difficult for the Soviet public to understand. How could an uninformed Christian fanatic win a Russian history contest? It would not fit the propaganda process that was a part of Moscow life. But all the same, Ivan thought, she did not have to pretend that he had refused.

But it seemed that all friendliness with his teacher was over. When her eyes met Ivan's gaze, she hardened her expression before continuing with the lessons for the rest of the class.

That was it. Ivan felt as if he were not in the class at all—that somehow everything she said was for the others, and he was simply an onlooker. When he raised his hand to offer an answer or to ask a question, he was ignored.

In the past, it had not been difficult to overlook the small spites of some of his classmates—his pencil deliberately broken if he left his seat or a foot stuck suddenly in the aisle as he walked to the chalk board.

But today, everything seemed to be going wrong. Vladimir Covich had given him a violent shove as the class stood for

Sophia Kutskova's entrance into the room. Ivan had lurched forward, almost falling on his desk and hitting his side on its sharp corner. He pulled in his muscles in pain.

As the class seated itself, Vladimir had whispered, "Aren't you supposed to bless me, Christian?"

Later, as Ivan stood in turn to recite for his teacher, someone had quietly lifted his inkwell from its place on his desk and poured a thin trickle of ink across his notebook. Ivan was certain Sophia Kutskova had seen it happening. How could she not have seen, since she had been looking at him as he answered? But she had said nothing. Ivan had had to stay in the classroom during his lunch hour to recopy his ink-smeared work. His stomach growled with hunger.

By late afternoon, Ivan was wondering if he were sick. He had a headache, and he could hardly force himself to do his work. He was afraid to raise his eyes from his desk and encounter the hard look of his teacher. His side ached. It seemed as if the slightest movement he made would provide an opportunity for some retaliation on the part of a classmate. If he reached for a book from the shelf under his seat, a swift ruler would knock it out of his hands. If someone passed his desk, he would be bumped, or a soft, insulting noise would be made.

Somehow it was Sophia Kutskova's fault. Her taunting him these last few days had seemed to unleash in the class a spirit of spite against Ivan that had never existed before. As the last bell rang, tears of relief sprang to his eyes. He was ashamed of how close to tears he had been all day.

There would be no waiting for Katya today. Ivan was going home, far away from school, as fast as he could. His heavy boots kicked a small spray of snow as he walked. Each step was that much further from the school. Abruptly he stopped, his way blocked by Vladimir Covich and several other classmates.

"Ivan Nazeroff?" Someone behind him called his name commandingly. Swiftly Ivan turned his head, and immediately felt a sharp blow on his temple. A look of astonishment spread over his face, and then one of pain as he was hit hard in the stomach and on the jaw at the same time. Books flying, he skidded in the slippery snow and awkwardly tried to regain his balance.

"You need to learn a lesson, Nazeroff." There seemed to be a voice close to his ear. "You need to learn that we won't put up with your reactionary ideas forever!" With the next blow, Ivan was down in the snow. A warm trickle of blood caught in his eyelashes and smeared his cheeks. The boys were on top of him, delivering blow upon blow. Ivan felt as if he were suffocating with pain and fear. He seemed to be coughing and crying and struggling against the weight of pounding bodies. His head swam in blackness.

9

Discovery

PYOTR'S VOICE was coming from a long way off. He was calling insistently, but Ivan was too tired to answer. He wanted only to be left to sleep. But the calling continued. Ivan would have to answer. He was gathering strength to respond, when he realized Pyotr was not calling him. He was calling Fyodor. Gratefully, Ivan sank back into oblivion, only to be roused by a hand roughly shaking his shoulder.

"Ivan! Ivan! Get up!" The voice had been calling him after all. He felt himself being pulled to his feet. Far-off pain made him open his eyes in bewilderment. The pain seemed to be spinning ever closer, like a hot meteor falling from the sky. Ivan groaned suddenly, as the meteor seemed to crash into his head.

"We'll help you, Ivan." Pyotr's voice was gruff with authority. "Can you walk?"

Ivan tried to answer. His mouth felt huge and unworkable. Finally he groaned an assent, the pain pounding at him as if it wanted release.

"What is this? You have been fighting, Ivan?" Sophia

71

Kutskova was out of breath, as if she had been running. She looked like a schoolgirl with her scarf wrapped so many times around her neck that it hid her chin. "You have been fighting, Ivan?"

"Sophia Kutskova, we just now found Ivan in the snow."

"It looks as if he got the worst of the fight," the teacher replied coolly. "Such conduct is not permitted, as he well knows. Bring him to the principal." She turned and slowly led the way back into the school and along the first floor corridor to the principal's office.

"I can walk alone," Ivan gasped to Pyotr. "Tell Sophia Kutskova I don't need help." He was feeling better, except for the hammering in his head, and he knew the boys would prefer to go home.

The principal invited him to sit down, an unusual gesture, and Ivan felt a surge of gratitude as he carefully lowered himself into the chair. Sophia Kutskova and the principal were talking quietly on the other side of the room. Finally the principal returned and looked gravely at Ivan. It was unfortunate that such a thing as a fight had occurred. The principal regretted that any students at Moscow School Number 17 would choose such unpeaceful methods of settling disputes. He would not ask Ivan to report the names of the other boys. But clearly, Ivan had been fighting. He would have to be punished. A week's suspension from school was decided upon, and Ivan was directed to return home immediately. This incident, along with other things (the principal glanced sympathetically at Sophia Kutskova) would go on Ivan's record. The principal hoped that a week's absence from school would give Ivan time to think about his conduct and resolve to improve.

The bus ride home, with every movement of the vehicle

shooting stabs of pain through Ivan's head and legs, the curious stares of people on the street—all seemed part of a dream to Ivan. Even the shock on his mother's face, the speed with which she got him into bed, and the cool cloths on his head and hot towels on his aching legs seemed unreal. Katya hovered by his bed, her eyes enormous with concern, until Momma called her away.

There was something bothering Ivan, something that kept emerging from the pain in his head. It was not the beating. Such things had happened to others before, and pain would go away. He remembered Pyotr's voice coming from a long distance.

"Ivan. Ivan! Get up." That was not it, it was something about Pyotr's voice. No! His face. It was the look in Pyotr's eyes as he bent over Ivan. It was the same cold look that he had seen in Sophia Kutskova's eyes. But Pyotr was his friend! In a rush, Ivan was in the schoolyard again, throwing snowballs at Pyotr. Pyotr's eyes had been unfriendly that day, too. His voice was insistent in Ivan's mind. "If you are not the informer, Ivan, why would your father be given his old job back?"

To Sophia Kutskova and his classmates, Ivan was an outsider because he was a despised Christian. To his old friends, Alexi, Fyodor and Pyotr, he was now an outsider because they thought him to be an informer. Loneliness worse than the pain swept over him. The informer had to be found! He closed his eyes, his thoughts swirling in a haze of hurt.

It seemed only a moment later that Momma was gently bathing his swollen face in warm water. She was dressed for work. Poppa had already left, and Katya was hovering behind Momma, her eyes rimmed with red. Ivan could not think why Katya had been crying.

"Praise to the Lord," Momma was saying, a soft smile playing around her mouth. "You slept all night, Ivan. I'm sorry to wake you, but Katya and I must leave soon."

A small tray with porridge and tea was on the table by his bed. Ivan tried to sit up. Pain in his shoulders and legs pushed him back against his pillow.

Katya gave a rueful smile. "To think the principal suspended you for a week, Ivan! As if you were not too injured to return!"

Momma was gently spooning porridge into Ivan's mouth. He shook his head and made another effort to lean on his arm. In his free hand he took the spoon and tried to swallow the cooled porridge. To please Momma, he drank some tea. She and Katya helped him to sit on the edge of the bed and finish the tea.

Ivan knew Momma wanted to stay home with him. But how could she explain such an absence at work? And Katya must go to school as usual. Enough attention had already been brought to the Nazeroff family.

They had been gone only a few minutes, and Ivan had tried experimentally to stand up for the first time, when a new thought came to him. Hockey! He would miss a week of practice. And would he be well enough to play even after a week? Even if the week's absence did not result in his being cut from the team?

The league games were about to start. They would pick the team and work out the plays before he returned. And even if they waited for him, he would be stiff and clumsy from his injuries. He would no longer be fast enough or good enough for the league games. Nickolai Fyodorovitch would make the most of his absence, Ivan knew. His chances to play that year were gone. Painfully lowering himself into bed, Ivan turned his face to the wall and wept.

The days at home passed very slowly. In the evenings, Ivan tried to respond cheerfully to the family's kind and playful attentions. He tried to make light of his losing the chance to play hockey in the league, but he knew no one was fooled.

But at night, when the lights were out and Ivan lay restlessly on his bed, or during the long days when he was alone in the apartment, the problem of the informer's identity haunted him.

The answer came one evening as he was lying on the couch in the living room. His muscles were still sore and his head ached if he moved rapidly, but he had spent the day working on his schoolwork (or at least what he imagined his class might be doing) and had felt well. He had not spent time turning over and over in his mind the question of the informer, as he had before. It was as if he had used up his quota of mental energy on that problem, and any attempt to return to it was met with a wall of mental rejection.

Their parents were visiting friends in the apartment building, and Katya was pouring some tea she had made. Ivan sat up so suddenly he made Katya spill the tea.

"Katya! It just came to me! I know who the informer is!" Instead of protesting the spilled tea, Katya stared at him excitedly.

"Ivan! Who?" The pool of tea on the tray cloth was slowly growing larger and larger. For the moment, Katya was unconcerned.

"Katya! It's so simple! Listen!" Ivan swung his stiff legs off the couch and leaned toward his sister.

"First, Fyodor left Alexi's house and was picked up by the

police. Later, I left, and they were waiting for me. Pyotr stayed for supper at Alexi's and then the police got him. They got Alexi last, after all had gone."

"I know all that!" Katya looked as if she would jump up and shake the information out of Ivan if he did not continue.

"But—" Ivan's voice lifted over his sister's, "when the police picked me up, they already had the paper with Scripture on it, and they knew that we had not simply been having a birthday party. They didn't bring the paper out until all the boys had been brought to the police station, but when they questioned me, they asked me if I knew what Jeremiah meant. They already had the paper before they questioned me!"

Katya's eyes were shocked. "That means Fyodor—"

"Yes! But *I'm* the only one who could know that for sure, because when you figure it out, the informer had to be either Fyodor or me, and it was not me!"

"You must tell Momma and Poppa."

Ivan sighed. He felt a pang of regret at telling Katya. "No! It couldn't do any good. They don't know that my friends think I am an informer. Knowing would only worry them, and they would be as helpless as you or I in trying to take the blame off of me."

Besides, something more was looming in Ivan's mind. In two days, he would have to return to the police station and give them his answer. This was a battle he had to fight alone.

10

In the Lion's Den

PERHAPS he had made a mistake in not telling Katya he had to return to the police station. The crowd of students was thinning along the edges of the schoolyard, and a feeling of alarm came over Ivan. What if the police kept him for a long time? Katya was his link with home, and he was letting her slip away!

"Katya!" He could see her waiting in a long line at the bus stop. She turned her head, pleased that he was looking for her. His feet flew along the sidewalk, skillfully avoiding bumping into people as he ran. Fear that the bus would whisk her away gave speed to his legs, which were still aching from the previous week's beating.

She made a place for him in the line. "It is so crowded today, you would think it was a holiday. Such long lines for the buses!"

Ivan was in a fever of impatience. "Katya! Listen. I have to go back to the police station for a little while."

His voice was low, but he could not resist a nervous glance over his shoulder. No one seemed to have heard.

Katya was frightened. "Ivan! What for? What has happened?"

"Nothing. Just listen. If I am late, you will know where I am. All right?" He turned swiftly.

"But wait, Ivan! Wait!" Katya could not leave her place in the long line to chase him for an answer. Gratefully, Ivan strode away. As he walked, he began to think about the radio sermon on Daniel in the lion's den.

It took him longer than he had expected to reach the police station. The streets were unusually full of people as he made his way through them, glad that he wasn't on the packed busses which lurched by.

The iron gate of the police station clanged behind him with a grating sound that reminded Ivan uncomfortably of prison cells. But there was nothing to be nervous about. A simple matter. He had only to tell the police captain that he did not wish to be an informer. He had done nothing wrong. But all the same, his heart began pounding wildly as he entered the large reception room of the police station and approached the desk.

The officer was writing rapidly. A phone was ringing. People were coming and going at a fast pace. Ivan's eyes strayed to a guard at the head of a corridor, whose drab green uniform was almost gray in the shadow. Slung over his shoulder, his rifle glinted in the pale electric light.

Finally the comrade officer at the desk lifted his eyes to Ivan. He looked annoyed.

"What is it, young comrade? We are busy today."

At that moment, Comrade Yakov stepped out of a room into the dim corridor and hurried to the front desk with a sheath of papers.

"I have an appointment with him—with the Comrade

80

Officer Yakov." Ivan looked appealingly at the officer, waiting to be recognized.

Yakov groaned. "I have no time today."

Ivan's heart leaped with joy. So the Lord would shut up the lion's mouth! But the next moment his hopes fell just as suddenly, as the officer said, "Never mind. Come to my office. Ah! What a day!"

Comrade Yakov stood at his desk looking at Ivan. His voice was impatient.

"Now, Ivan Nazeroff, you have had a week to think over my offer. And are you tired of your friends blaming you unjustly for being an informer? And I would wish for them they could be of such a service to Mother Russia! Have you found out that the love that you fanatics talk about doesn't go very far?"

Ivan spoke carefully. "I think, comrade, that there *is* real love among Christians, even though it doesn't seem—"

"No! It *doesn't* 'seem'! But I am very busy this afternoon. Shall I simply assume, then, that an intelligent young man like you has decided to prove himself a good citizen, and as a result enjoy all the benefits of our glorious revolution?"

A car started suddenly in the street outside the window. Ivan paled. It had sounded, for a moment, like a lion's roar.

Taking a full breath, Ivan chose his words as carefully as possible.

"I am sorry, comrade officer. I cannot become an informer. And in truth, there would be nothing to tell you. Believers do nothing against the Soviet Union or against the laws of our country—"

Yakov groaned in anger. A small nerve twitched in his cheek. "Ivan Nazeroff, I do not have *time* this afternoon for this kind of talk. You have been given a tremendous opportunity. Yet you spurn it. You were involved in an illegal meeting, yet no fine was placed upon your parents. We were willing to overlook what happened because of your age. Certainly we expect you to come to your senses—"

An officer in full uniform poked his head in the door and took in the scene. Comrade Yakov nodded as if in response to a command. The officer disappeared.

"You are making a very serious mistake." He paused, apparently more irritated than ever at Ivan's silence. "Today, of all days, I do not have time to discuss the fate of one stupid boy. Do you realize there has been a breakdown in our great Moscow subway system—something electrical—and the trains on one line have stopped? Transportation is critical. I am needed elsewhere. Yet you stand here and waste my time."

A phone was ringing in the distance. Ivan could hear hurried voices. Comrade Yakov looked furious for a second, then barked, "Go home!"

A joyful relief flooded Ivan.

"And go quickly, before I make you wait here all night!"

His steps clicked rapidly down the corridor. Ivan stood for a second in the dim afternoon light. His hands were still clenched nervously at his side. A slow smile broke upon his face, as with a sudden happy movement he wound his woolen scarf around his neck. He made his way, hands in pockets, through the large reception room and past the officer at the desk, now almost hidden by a commotion of milling police.

Even in the lion's den! Ivan was exulting as he made his way through the ever more congested streets. *Even in the lion's den, the Lord kept me safe.*

Arriving home, Ivan at last could tell his parents all about the troubles and doubts he had gone through in the past few days. His words tumbled out joyously as he told how good God had been to him.

What could one do, but celebrate, Momma and Poppa decided. It was a bad thing that Ivan had not told them about the police asking him to inform. This was too heavy a burden for a boy to have borne alone. And going to the police station almost without telling them! What if something had happened?

Ivan let Momma scold, careful not to remind her that even if she and Poppa had known, there was nothing they could have done to protect him. There was no law to which they could have appealed that would have restrained the police. He could have been sent away to a state school for reeducation. If Momma wanted to pretend that perhaps parents could do something to help their children, let her pretend.

Poppa kept shaking his head in pleasure and praising God for the breakdown of the subway system.

"If the officer had not been so busy with the transportation problems, he might have kept you at the station for hours. Perhaps overnight. He might have! To think how the Lord protected you! To think how it was this day, and no other, that it happened that you had to go! Praises! Praises to God!"

Ivan felt almost as giddy as Katya, who was whirling about the apartment, perching for a moment on a chair or on the couch and leaping up, hugging Ivan until he insisted he had had the last hug he would endure.

Later, as the family sat around the large table in the living room drinking steaming glasses of tea and hungrily eating the white bread and butter Momma passed, they began to piece together the events of the past weeks.

Poppa spoke slowly with good humor, as if he were talking

about characters in a book he had read and not about injustice to himself.

"When I was reported at the factory, my records were studied. I think it was clear to the police that I had done nothing wrong and that the man who reported me was lying. But it was, after all, an opportunity to ask me questions and to show me that those who are Christians are not friends of the state."

Katya choked on her bread. "Even though you love our country and have served faithfully in the army!"

Poppa shook a finger at her, smiling playfully. "Oh, that was very long ago, Katychka. That no longer counts."

Momma took the story up. "When you would not answer questions about other Christians, it was thought that perhaps your son could be made useful."

"Yes!" Poppa seemed to be enjoying a game. "But Ivan needed to be unhappy with the believers. Perhaps the police thought that if they could make Ivan angry at the other believers, he would cross over to help the police."

Ivan felt a rather unpleasant sensation of surprise in realizing he had been the center of police attention. "When the police discovered that I had been at a Bible study, they planned a way to encourage me to inform. By giving back your old job at the factory, Poppa, it would look as if I *had* informed, and the others would be suspicious of me."

"Which is exactly what happened." Katya was biting with enthusiasm into her second piece of soft, white bread.

Momma smiled a slow smile. "Except that you did not agree to inform for them, Vanya." She used her pet name for him and teasingly rumpled his hair.

"But there is something I do not understand." Poppa rubbed his head reflectively. "Why did the police *want* Ivan to inform for them? If Fyodor is an informer, as Ivan believes, there would be no need to have two informers in our small group of believers."

The family fell silent. It was a good question. But then, the ways of the police were past finding out.

11

Restored Friendships

NOW THAT the dreaded police interview was in the past, Ivan wanted to start life afresh. After an examination in school, one went the next day to a new section of material, perhaps a new textbook. At least one began a new page in one's notes. It was satisfying to be able to put the old behind, and to begin anew. But life was not like that.

Unfortunately, Ivan was greatly behind in his work. The week of suspension had done more than remove him from the hockey team. (And the coach had looked at him with a strange sadness when he had said good-bye.) The week had resulted in Ivan's missing an astonishing amount of classwork. Sophia Kutskova offered him no help in getting caught up. She ignored his return and continued to overlook his raised hand in the question period following the lectures.

He wondered who had been chosen as the class candidate for the all-Moscow essay contest. Perhaps Sonya Sorina. She was very good in history, Ivan knew. Her thick braids bent over her books told him nothing.

In spare moments during the day, Ivan thought about Fyodor. What good would it do to confront him with the knowledge that he was the informer? Surely he would deny it.

And to tell the truth, Ivan admitted to himself, it was very difficult to believe such a thing of Fyodor. The boys and their families had been friends for many years. Every year Fyodor's family had gone with Ivan's family in the spring for an Easter service in the forests outside of Moscow. Ivan was stabbed by the memory of Fyodor slushing through the snowy mud, embarrassed by his too-large boots. How they had teased him!

His mother was a courageous woman. Once a week, in the evening after work, a small group of women gathered in her home under the pretense of attending an embroidery club. They would sit, needles flashing in the lamplight, singing hymns and sharing Bible verses and praying for one another.

It was difficult to believe Fyodor could have informed.

"Ivan Nazeroff?"

Ivan was trying to button his coat with one hand, holding his books in the other arm. He turned in surprise at the friendly tone. Sonya Sorina waited shyly, while the rest of the class streamed out of the room, happy to be gone.

"We get the same bus, Ivan. May I walk and talk with you?"

The crowded halls made talking impossible, and they walked together without trying to communicate until they were outside. Ivan glimpsed Alexi and Fyodor hurrying ahead of them. Fyodor cast a look over his shoulder at Ivan, then turned quickly back. Ivan was shocked at his face. Fyodor looked very tired. Perhaps sick.

Ivan's guess about Sonya had been correct. Sophia Kutskova had chosen her as the competition candidate. Sonya's red neck scarf had been caught in the collar of her coat when she put it on, and it seemed to point accusingly at Ivan.

She had been working on her essay, but she was concerned about it. It was against the contest rules for her to ask the advice of her teacher. But would Ivan read it? She smiled hopefully as she stepped up into the bus ahead of him.

"Of course!" Ivan tried to be generous. It would have been wonderful if he could have entered the contest. He knew how proud Momma and Poppa would have been of him, even if he had not won. But Daniel had not given in to the wrong wishes of his government, and God had blessed him. Would not God bless Ivan, too?

"Of course, Sonya!" This time Ivan smiled eagerly. "I am not sure that you need any help from me, but if you have your essay with you, I'll take it home and read it tonight." Ivan was enjoying talking to a classmate again.

Sonya glanced quickly at Ivan, then down at her gloved hands in her lap. "I'm sorry about what happened to you, Ivan. I mean the beating. It was cruel of the boys to do that, and you were very good not to tell who did it. Many students in the class admire you for not telling and for not trying to pay them back."

Ivan stared at Sonya in disbelief. Could it be true that he had friends in the class? His voice was low. "I thought everyone was angry at me because I don't wear the red scarf and because I could not enter the contest."

Sonya smiled again. "Lenin himself said that there would be freedom of religion in Russia. I do not believe in any god, Ivan, but I know that it is not according to Lenin to be unjust to those who do. Others feel this way. You will see."

That evening, Momma brought out her embroidery and sat at the table with Ivan and Katya as they did their homework.

89

Poppa was in his chair, listening to music on the radio and reading. It was a quiet scene, and Ivan raced through page after page of homework, invigorated as he had not been since the first day his father had returned early from work with the news of his dismissal from the factory.

Momma's voice broke the silence. "I was at Fyodor's house last evening. It was our Bible study."

Katya and Ivan's pens stopped in midsentence.

"I was telling the Christian sisters about Ivan and how the police had tried to persuade him to be an informer. And how he had refused." Her eyes rested with a soft pride on Ivan's startled face. "Why should I not tell?"

"But Fyodor's *momma?* You talked to her about informers?" Ivan marvelled.

"She does not know, Ivan, if Fyodor *did* inform on your Bible study at Alexi's. All the women rejoiced for you, Ivan. And so did I."

Momma bent her head over her sewing, and said no more.

In later years, Ivan was to remember the next morning as a shower of white. Snow was falling as he stood on the cold floor by his bed, and the window was white with frost, with only the top of the pane clear enough for him to see the huge swirling flakes outside.

Momma had a simple white cloth on the breakfast table, and Katya's fresh face above her thick white sweater smiled over the bread and tea. The winter light in the room was bright.

They had all been surprised at the early pounding on the door. Poppa had left for the factory, but Momma, getting ready to leave for work herself, pulled open the door in astonishment. Covered in a thick layer of light snow stood Alexi, Pyotr, and Fyodor, smiling shyly and asking to come in.

It was a few minutes before the boots were pulled off, the coats shaken in the hall, and the boys sitting at the table, glasses of amber tea warming their red fingers.

Katya sat dumbfounded at this unexpected visit, her eyes straying to Fyodor's face and moving away at the warning in her mother's eyes. There was laughing and what Katya called "warming up talk" and then a stillness fell over the group.

Fyodor cleared his throat. He was looking at Ivan. "I've come, Ivan, to tell you I have done you a great wrong. I—I confessed this wrong to my family last night, and to the families of Pyotr Kachenko and Alexi Petrovitch. They have forgiven me."

He shifted in his chair. "It was I who informed on the meeting at Alexi's. I permitted you to be blamed for it, and I was afraid to speak up. Although I didn't mean it, my silence led the police to try to make you an informer and caused you much suffering. I am asking a very great thing of you. I am asking you to forgive me."

Many times Ivan had seen his father embrace a Christian friend. It was the Russian way. They would fling their outstretched arms around each other, slapping each other's backs, their faces wreathed in smiles. Never before had Ivan felt so much like a Russian.

In a moment he was on his feet. Seeing the smile on his face, Fyodor stood uncertainly by his chair. In a huge embrace, Ivan threw his arms around his friend.

"Thank you, Fyodor! Thank you for telling me. All is well now."

Fyodor tried to brush away the tears that were brimming

in his eyes. Momma was gently blowing her nose on the lace-edged handkerchief that she always kept in her sleeve but never seemed to use.

Fyodor was talking rapidly.

"It was all an accident, from the very beginning. When I came out of Alexi's, the police picked me up. They knew about my Momma's Bible studies and wanted to ask me questions. I thought that somehow they had found out about *our* meeting and were questioning me about that. When I got to the police station, I was confused trying to answer about the birthday party. What made everything worse was that the paper, with the verses of Scripture on it, was in my pocket with my gloves. I must have put my gloves on top of the paper and then picked it up with them and put the paper and my gloves in my pocket together. To think of how we looked for it!"

Ivan began to laugh. It was silly to think about. Soon the boys and then Katya and Momma were laughing.

"When I was about to leave the police station, I took my gloves out of my pocket. Out fell the paper. The police read it and then made me take off my coat again. I had already told the names of those at the birthday party."

"As did I," Ivan assured him.

"So that is how it all came to be. After it happened, I was a coward not to tell the truth about it. But I made myself think it didn't matter. My parents will explain everything to the believers at church, Ivan. No one will think of you as an informer again."

Alexi slapped Fyodor on the back. "Nor are you an informer, Fyodor! It was not intended."

"No! It was not." Fyodor looked so fierce, Katya thought she would laugh again. "They did try to make me agree to